Kindred
Souls

Patricia MacLachlan

Kindred Souls

SCHOLASTIC INC.

In memory of my father—
born in a sod house on the prairie he loved
—P.M.

ISBN 978-0-545-55539-5

12 11 10 9 8 7 6 5 4 3 2   13 14 15 16 17 18/0

Printed in the U.S.A.   40

First Scholastic printing, January 2013

Typography by Jennifer Rozbruch

Contents

1

The Talk of Birds

My grandfather, Billy, hears the talk of birds. He leans out the open bedroom window with his head tilted to listen in the warm prairie morning.

He tells me the hummingbirds outside speak to him in short, brisk sentences when they fly quickly up and down and around the hanging feeders of sugar water.

"Red-tailed hawk, too," announces Billy at the open window of his room. Billy lives with us on the farm that used to be his.

I hear a high whistle outside.

"You can't see that hawk," I say.

Billy smiles. This is our daily joke.

"He's talking to me. Don't need to see him," says Billy.

"What's he saying?"

"'Good day, old man,' he says. 'Still alive, I see.'"

Billy is eighty-eight years old, and I don't worry about him dying. He will live forever. I know that.

"That redtail isn't eighty-eight years old," I

tell him. "You can't have been talking to *him* all these years."

"Nope. Talked to his father and mother before him, and all his ancestors way back to the first bird of time," says Billy.

I look at Billy's large gnarled hands and his wrinkled face and his bush of white hair. I believe him when he says he talked to the first bird of time.

He lives in a sunny room that looks up to the slough that is empty in the summer and filled with water and ducks in the fall. It is a small piece of his old life, like the big prairie that spreads out around is a big piece of his old life.

The day is sunny, and Papa is cutting hay in the far field. His tractor goes around and around, birds flying behind him as he sends up insects and seeds. After the hay dries, my older brother, Jesse, and my sister, Lida, will gather it into windrows for baling. Sometimes I see Lida working by the barn, her corn-colored hair catching the light as she moves.

"Funny sound, that tractor," says Billy. "We used to plow with horses."

"Named . . . ," I prompt him.

"Wendell and Jack and Juno and . . ." Billy stops.

"Jake!" I say, laughing, because that is my name.

"Ah yes, Jake," says Billy, pretending he has forgotten.

Mama comes into the room with folded laundry.

"Want a cup of tea, Billy?" she asks, opening and closing drawers.

Everyone has always called Grandfather Billy, even Mama. Lida and Jesse, too. Jesse calls him Billy the Kid when Billy isn't listening. Except for my grandmother. When Grandmother Lou was alive, she called him Lamb Chop.

"Tea! You know how I feel about tea, Lottie. I smell that coffee in the kitchen," says Billy.

Mama smiles at me.

"How many cups of coffee have you had this morning?"

"Seventeen," says Billy quickly.

Mama laughs.

"You know that's not true. I guess one more cup won't hurt you." Mama goes to the kitchen for a cup of coffee for Billy.

"What are you doing home instead of at school?" asks Billy.

"It's summer, Billy."

"Oh . . . so it is. We used to get off school to work in the fields."

"Well, now I get off school in the summer to spend time with you."

Billy turns to look at me, his eyes sharp blue. He smiles. "Yes, there's that," he says softly, putting his hard old hand over mine. "There's that."

We are quiet. I love the feel of his hand.

Outside, the hummingbirds flash silently in the sunlight.

2

The Walk

After I do my chores, Billy and I take our daily walk around the farm. Every day I'm not in school we take the same walk. It isn't boring. It is peaceful and what Billy calls "predictable."

"I like predictable," says Billy. "I like spring rain. I like summer heat. I like thunderstorms with lightning all around. I like the wind and snow of winter."

"That's because you don't have to walk to school in wind and snow," I tell him.

"Aha! See?" says Billy. "You're predictable, too!"

We visit the cows, and Billy speaks to them in a sweet voice.

"Girls? How goes the day, girls? Rosie, you're looking pretty big, and Betsy and Lizzie? And you, Chico?" he says to our bull. "Enough green grass?"

We visit the horses, and Billy feeds them carrots and rubs their necks and they lean on him.

And then we go where we always end our

walk. We go to the place where Billy was born on this farm. Up the rise and higher up the hill to the edge of the slough is the granary. Nearby is a spring.

We stop in front of the Russian olive bushes: five of them, clumped and thick and silvery. Taller than Billy.

When Billy pushes the branches of one bush aside, there it is. A small wall of prairie grass and mud three feet high. And Billy says what he always says, has always said for all the years I've known him.

"I loved that sod house."

He says it softly. I could say it with him, I have heard it so often.

I smile. Billy smiles, too.

Sometimes our talk changes a little. Like today.

"It must have been cold in winter," I say.

"Oh no, there was a woodstove there," says Billy quickly. "And a beautiful red rug on the dirt floor. And"——he peers at me and sits on a big rock——"you know about the windows."

"Yes. When you were a little boy, you put cans and packages on the windowsills and pretended it was the store."

"I did."

It is very quiet then. A wind comes up and rustles the leaves of the Russian olive bushes.

And then Billy says what he always says at

the end of the conversation.

"I miss that sod house," he says very softly.

The wind blows his white hair. And he sits until finally I hand him his cane.

He looks surprised. He smiles at me and gets up.

"I miss that sod house," he says again.

And we walk down the hill, away from the slough, past the granary, past the barn, until we are home again.

3

Lucy

It is the evening, dusk really—just before the hummingbirds have their last drinks of sugar water—when something unpredictable happens. The dog appears.

Billy sees the dog first.

"Well, look here," he says.

"Where?"

"By the barn. Give me my cane, Jake."

I look out quickly and see a black-and-white dog, smallish, sitting close to the barn, looking at Billy's window.

Together we walk through the kitchen.

"What's up?" Mama says.

"Can't tell yet," says Billy. "But we'll let you know."

Mama smiles. Mama always smiles at Billy.

We go out on the porch. The dog is still there, sitting calmly. We walk down the steps and across the yard. We can hear the tractor making a last round. Soon Papa will head to the barn.

The dog stands up when we get closer.

"Well, you came," says Billy, as if he's been

expecting the dog.

I walk closer and the dog backs up a bit.

"Stand back, Jake," says Billy.

Billy hands me his cane and walks toward the dog. The dog sits and waits for him.

"The dog doesn't like me," I say.

"Just likes me better," says Billy. "That's all."

"Well, hello, girl." He speaks so softly, I can hardly hear him.

The dog noses his outstretched hand. Then she moves over and leans against Billy.

Behind us the door opens, and Mama walks out to the porch. She wipes her hands on a towel.

The dog looks at her and stays with Billy.

"Billy. What is that?" she says.

Billy laughs.

"I think she's a dog, Lottie," he says.

"You know what I mean," Mama says. "What's he doing here?"

"She," corrects Billy. "This is Lucy. My dog," he calls.

"I just named her," he whispers to me as he reaches for the cane.

"Wait," says Mama. "Are you going to bring her in the house?"

"I am," says Billy, walking more quickly now because of his cane.

He stops and looks very hard at Mama.

"I am," he repeats. "This is my house, too," he says in a soft voice. He doesn't say it in a mean way. But it is clear and strong.

Mama lifts her shoulders in a sigh.

"Okay. But she'd better not pee in the house."

Billy and Lucy walk past me toward the house. Billy beckons for me to follow.

"We'll both pee outside if you want, Lottie," Billy says.

Mama begins to laugh. Billy laughs, too. And as we walk to the house and up the steps, Lucy gives me a sideways look as if to say, *My house, too, don't you know.*

Lucy sits by Billy's chair when we eat dinner. She doesn't beg for food. She doesn't whine. She just sits as if it is her place and always has been.

"I think she's beautiful," says Lida. "What kind is she?"

"I'll look it up in the encyclopedia," says Billy.

Jesse laughs.

"That book is so old that there are probably new breeds by now!"

Billy puts down his fork and stares at Jesse.

"That book is as old as I am," he says in a low voice.

My brother gets quiet.

"I didn't mean anything bad," he says.

"That's good," says Billy with a smile.

"You know, we'd better check to see if anyone has lost a dog," says Mama.

"I've never seen that dog anywhere around the fields or in town, Charlotte," says Papa. He's the only one who calls Mama by her full name: Charlotte.

Papa takes a piece of chicken from his plate and offers it to Lucy. Very gently, she takes the bite of chicken and eats it.

"Nope. She's not from around here. She is my dog. She came to me," says Billy.

Jesse looks at Billy as if he's crazy.

Jesse should know better.

Lucy came to Billy.

She's his dog.

Billy is eighty-eight years old.

And Billy is going to live forever.

4

A Piece of Sod

It's another sunny morning. Billy is drinking his second cup of coffee in the kitchen. Lucy eats leftover eggs in a blue bowl.

"She has some Border collie," says Jesse, looking up at Billy. He shows Billy the picture in the book. "Probably a mix."

Billy nods as if he knows this. Lucy looks at Jesse as if she knows this, too.

"I think you're right, Jesse," Billy says, getting up and lifting his cane off the back of his chair. Lucy looks up from her bowl.

"Finish eating, Lucy," says Billy, waiting.

Lucy licks the bowl and then stands next to Billy.

Papa smiles and gets up, too.

"A new chum, Billy," he says.

"We're walking," Billy announces.

Lucy and Billy walk to the door. Billy waves his hand to us without turning around. I feel a sudden pang of something different. Billy's going off without me. He and I always walk the farm together.

Billy turns.

"Coming, Jake?"

I jump up from the table. Lida gets up to go, too.

"Lida, your turn to wash dishes and clean up," says Mama.

"Because I'm a girl, right?" complains Lida.

Mama laughs.

"Because you're a family member," she says.

"I washed yesterday," says Billy. "And I'm no girl."

"Plate in the sink, please," says Mama to me.

I quickly pick up my plate and Billy's cup and put them in the sink.

"And we're off!" says Billy.

"Lucy can wash tomorrow," says Mama.

I watch Lucy look back. *Can a dog smile?* I think Lucy smiles.

We walk through the yard to the cows. Lucy walks and runs, nose to the ground, circling around us but always staying close to Billy.

"This is Lucy, girls," says Billy. "That's Chico," Billy says to Lucy.

Chico and the cows back up and roll their eyes at Lucy.

Lucy makes a snuffing sound.

"She's clearing her nose to smell them," says Billy. "Animals do that."

The horses ignore Lucy, pushing on Billy's pockets for carrots.

We walk up the hill until we come to the

Russian olive bushes. Billy is tired. He sits on the big rock and hands me his cane.

"Where I was born," he says to Lucy.

She tilts her head at him. Then she walks around the bushes, sniffing. She disappears into the bushes, and I can hear her rummaging around.

"What's she up to?" asks Billy with a smile.

I lean the cane on the rock by Billy and crawl into the bushes. Lucy is digging. She turns to lick my face, making me laugh. She paws something loose. I pick it up.

I duck back out from the bushes.

"It's this." I hold up a cut brick of sod and grass.

Billy looks at it for a minute before he reaches and takes it. He looks out over the slough and the huge prairie. The sky is very blue, and only two big clouds hang there.

"My sod house. A piece of it." His voice is low.

"No one took care of it after we finally had enough money to build the wood house."

He turns and points his cane at our farmhouse.

There is a silence then. Billy looks down at the brick in his hand. I know Billy is remembering something from long ago.

"My mama sang lullabies to me in the sod house," he says. "She sat in that old rocking chair in my room and sang lullabies."

And he sings:

Hush, little baby, don't say a word,
Mama's going to buy you a mockingbird.
If that mockingbird won't sing,
Mama's going to buy you a diamond ring.

Billy's voice is soft and steady. And nice. But I don't want him to sing anymore. I don't want him to remember things that make him sad anymore.

I take the brick and turn it over in my hand.

"How hard is it to cut a brick of sod?" I ask, surprising myself.

Billy stops looking out at the prairie and looks at me.

He smiles brightly.

"You could do it," says Billy. "You could!"

"What?"

"You could," Billy says again.

He turns and begins to walk back down the hill. He is walking fast.

I run to catch up with him.

"And I am going to teach you how to build a sod house," he says, not looking at me. "I'll tell you everything. And then . . ." He pauses. "And then you can build me a sod house. A little one."

I stop, but Billy and Lucy keep walking.

"But what if I don't want to build a sod house?" I call after him.

"You will," Billy calls back to me.

"Why?"

"Because we're kindred souls, you and I," calls Billy.

He begins to sing his lullaby again. Now it is peppy and fast, not slow and soft, like the way he sang it before.

Hush, little baby, don't say a word
Mama's going to buy you a mockingbird.

Not me, I think. *I don't want to build a sod house. Why would I ever, ever want to build a sod house? Why did I even ask him how hard it was to build?*

Billy walks, his white hair bright in the sun.

And what's a "kindred soul"?

5

Kindred Souls

I'm in Jesse's room. It is book lined and dark, the only light the flickering light of Jesse's computer screen. I'm always surprised at the books. Jesse loves books. He has all the books he read when he was little. He uses his money from summer work and farm chores to buy books.

Jesse turns around to stare at me.

"He wants *what*?"

I nod my head.

"What I told you. A sod house. A little one," I add.

Jesse laughs.

"You're just a kid! You're only ten! What's that old coot thinking?"

"Look it up, Jesse," I say. "Please."

"He's old and nuts. You're young and nuts," says Jesse.

"He says we're kindred souls," I tell him.

"Ha!"

I sit down on Jesse's bed. I look around the room at all the books.

"You read all these," I say, waving my hand. "I know you understand."

32

Jesse stares at me for a long time. Then he smiles slightly. He gets up and goes to the bookshelves and takes down a book.

"Here. Look it up."

The book is old and worn. *How to Build a Sod House* is the title.

"Read that," he says. "It used to belong to Billy."

He turns back to the computer as if ignoring me.

"Kindred souls," he says to himself with a laugh.

I go to the door to leave.

"I'll look it up on the computer," he says softly.

I turn to smile at him, but he is typing

on his computer.

He doesn't even know when I leave.

The book is old, with yellow, brittle pages. I look at the pictures first: farmers cutting sod, piling one brick on top of another, no trees in sight. There are women in long skirts, children and chickens nearby scattered across the yards, family dogs sitting there. I think of Lucy. Any one of these dogs could be Lucy.

It gets darker, and I turn on the light and lie down on the bed with the book.

"Jake?"

Mama whispers to me, and I wake up

34

quickly as if she has yelled, the book falling to the floor. She leans down to pick it up. She leafs through the book, then hands it back to me.

"It's late, Jake. Almost midnight."

I yawn.

"Billy told me," she says.

There's a silence then, the only sound the wind outside my open window.

"You don't have to do this," she says.

"I'm not going to do it."

Mama walks to the door.

"Why do you sound angry?" she asks.

I shake my head.

"You know," she says, turning. The light in

the hallway shines through her hair.

"When you were born, Billy loved you right away. When I see the two of you together . . ." She takes a breath. "Sometimes I think you were born for him."

I look up, but she is gone.

And I know. I know that I'm not really angry. I am afraid. Afraid that I can't build the sod house that Billy wants so much.

I turn out my bedside light. Then I turn it on again, and put the sod house book under my pillow and turn off the light again.

Kindred souls.

All I hear is the wind.

6

Birth and Death

On the last day of August, in a wild rainstorm, Rosie the cow has a calf.

"I didn't know she was going to calf," I say to Papa, looking out the window.

He has just come in dripping, his hair plastered to his head.

"Well, *she* knew," says Papa with a smile, taking a towel from Mama to dry his hair.

"Always in the rain," says Mama.

"Always," says Billy at the kitchen table. "You know why?"

Billy is looking at me, but it is Lida who answers.

"Predators," she says. "Coyotes or wolves. The rainwater washes off the scent, so it is safer for the calf."

Billy nods at Lida.

Lida is the expert on farming, both machinery and animals. She keeps the animals healthy and the tractor in working order.

"We lost lots of calves to coyotes early on," Billy says with that faraway look he gets, remembering. "Birth and death. Close together on a farm," he says. "Very close," he adds in a soft voice.

Mama looks up at Billy and then at Papa.

"The calf is in the barn," Papa says.

Lida takes Papa's hat off the hook by the door and puts it on, then her rain slicker.

"I'll go make sure," she says. "The wind is picking up."

"Wait for me!"

I grab my coat and rain hat.

Together Lida and I run through the yard, the wind whipping around us. Suddenly my hat blows off, tumbling across the yard. I chase after it and can hear Lida laughing. I almost fall in the mud as we open the large wooden paddock gate.

"Look," says Lida.

She takes my arm and pulls me into the barn. It is quiet all of a sudden. The smell of hay and animals fills the air.

Lida points.

There is Rosie, staring at us warningly. Next to her, almost under her belly, is the calf, beautiful and clean, with a white face and ears.

The other cows and Chico are at the back of the barn.

"Rosie is keeping the rest of them away," says Lida.

"Oh," I say. "Oh, look at you," I whisper.

I kneel down, trying to get closer, but

Rosie moves in front of her calf.

"You'll have to wait until she gets used to having the calf," says Lida. "Rosie's protective."

Lida scoops out some grain from the grain bin. She drops some in front of Rosie. The other cows look over and start moving toward us.

"Oops," says Lida. "Have to feed the crowd."

She takes grain to the rest of the cows in the back of the barn. Then she drops down and peers at the calf closely.

"A boy," she says.

I smile at Lida in the warm, dry, sweet-smelling barn.

"A boy," I repeat.

"Well?"

Billy looks up from the kitchen table as we rush out of the rain into the house.

"A boy," Lida says.

Billy grins.

"Billy," he says.

"What?" I ask.

"Billy," he repeats. "I want to name him Billy. That means there will be a Billy around here for a long time."

There is a sudden silence in the room.

"But you're Billy. And you're here for a long time," I say to him.

"Not forever," says Billy. "I shall pass out of

the picture one day. I plan to do so."

I look quickly at the portrait of us all, hanging over the fireplace.

"He doesn't mean that picture, Jake," whispers Jesse.

I know that, and Jesse's whisper brings tears to my eyes.

"No," I say, ignoring Jesse and Billy.

Billy reaches out and takes my hand.

"No," I say again.

Billy's hand is dry.

"There will be no worrying here," says Billy. "You hear?"

He says it very quietly, as if he's saying it to me alone, but I know everyone else can hear.

I swallow and nod.

"There will be no worrying. There will be great joy because we have a new calf named . . . Billy!"

We all call out "Billy" together, and I can't help smiling. Billy does that to me, even though, if he asked, I would tell him I am not full of joy.

It's dark. Everyone has gone to bed. My bedroom door is open. I always sleep with it wide-open so I can hear Billy. I hear the clicking of Lucy's nails on the wood floor and a sudden sound that I know is Lucy jumping up onto Billy's bed.

When I look up, Jesse is leaning against the door frame.

"What?" I ask.

"You know, you may as well go along with Billy. He is powerful. You can't change some things." Jesse clears his throat and looks embarrassed.

"I know. There are some things you can't change. No matter how hard you want to."

And then Jesse is gone. He appears and disappears like Mama. I almost imagine I can see the outline of where he stood. In Billy's room Lucy yawns a loud dog yawn.

I close my eyes.

Maybe I'll do it.

7

Chickie

"So," says Billy at the kitchen table, "we had a sod cutter like this."

He points to the picture in the book: a farmer standing by some horses, getting ready to pull the cutter. Lucy lays at his feet, her eyes looking steadily at Billy.

Lida nods. "I've seen those in old barns. Rubin has one, I think. You could ask Rubin."

Rubin is our neighbor a mile away. Sometimes he still uses horses for some garden plowing because he loves his horses.

"Nope," says Billy. "It's you I'm asking."

"You need the right grass, you know," says Lida. "Buffalo grass, or wheatgrass."

"Yes," says Billy. "Or what we have out there. Indian grass."

Billy leans back and grins at Lida. "And you," he says, "can learn how to cut the sod."

Lida sighs and looks sideways at me. "I'm not saying I'll do it, Billy," she says. "But I'll study it."

"That's good," says Billy. "Jake will need that."

I stare at Billy. I feel my face get hot.

"I didn't really ever say I'd build a sod house!" I say. My voice is loud in the room.

Billy rubs his head as if it hurts.

Lucy whines.

"Jake," warns Mama.

"That's right," says Billy. "You didn't say you would."

He stands up. He holds on to the table for a moment.

"You all right, Billy?" asks Mama.

"Tired."

Mama puts her hand on Billy's forehead.

"You have a temperature!" she says. "You're hot."

Mama makes Billy sit down. He is so much

48

taller than Mama, but she sits him down as if he's a child. Lucy sits up and puts her head on Billy's leg.

"Lida. Call Doctor Miller. The number is on the refrigerator."

"No," says Billy. "I don't want her. She's bossy."

"So are you," says Mama. "And you flirt with her every time you see her!"

"That's because she's beautiful," says Billy. "But bossy."

Mama sits next to Billy and puts her arm around him and kisses him on his cheek.

"So are you," Mama repeats softly.

An hour later Dr. Miller gets to the house. She is little and cheerful, with black hair. Billy is in bed with Lucy. I'm sitting next to the bed. Mama rocks in the rocking chair Billy's mother brought from far away.

"A new calf!" she says happily as she comes into Billy's bedroom. "And I see a dog."

"Hello, Chickie," says Billy.

"Stop flirting," says Dr. Miller, laughing. "I'm a professional doctor."

Dr. Miller pats Lucy, and Lucy wags her tail.

"The calf is named Billy," I tell her. "Billy named him."

"I see," says Dr. Miller.

"This is Lucy," says Billy.

Dr. Miller takes out her stethoscope.

"Everyone else can leave. Open your shirt, Billy."

"Lucy stays," says Billy.

"Lucy stays," repeats Dr. Miller.

"I'm not really sick, you know," we hear Billy say as we leave to stand in the hall.

"Then you won't need me," says Dr. Miller.

"What do you know about sod houses, Chickie?" asks Billy.

"Stop talking. I'm listening to your chest."

In the hallway I start to cry.

"I yelled at Billy," I whisper to Mama. "I've never yelled at Billy before. Ever."

Mama reaches over and takes my hand.

"It's my fault," I say.

"It's all right, Jake. Billy doesn't care."

She pulls me into her arms until Dr. Miller comes out to tell us that Billy has bronchitis.

"I'd feel better if he were in the hospital, but he won't go unless Lucy can go. I'm worried about pneumonia. I'll come by tomorrow morning. Please call if he has any trouble breathing. He needs rest and medicine."

"He needs chicken soup," says Mama.

They are both wrong and I know it.

I finally know it. He has told me. He has told us all. And now he has talked about it to Dr. Miller.

What Billy needs is a sod house.

8

Billy's Rule

Lucy won't leave Billy's bed. She keeps watch while he sleeps, and watches him when he takes his medicine and eats chicken soup. Sometimes when I look in his bedroom, Billy is sleeping with his hand on Lucy's head. Billy doesn't talk much. That's how I can tell he's really sick. He never once talks about the sod house. He's pale and doesn't get out of bed very much the next day, except for once when I find him looking out the window to the slough.

Today I stand at his doorway, watching him breathe.

"Jake?"

I jump.

Billy doesn't open his eyes, but he knows I'm there.

"Take Lucy out, will you? She won't leave the bed."

"Sure, Billy."

"Lucy, Lucy."

I call softly, but Lucy just looks at me.

Billy smiles.

"You'll have to take her," he says.

I take Lucy by her collar, and she jumps off the bed. She turns once to look at Billy, then follows me down the hallway, through the kitchen, and out into the yard.

It's clear and warm, with no clouds in the sky. Too sunny for me. I shade my eyes and watch Papa's tractor in the fields. Lida comes out of the barn, and she shades her eyes, too. I look up at the clump of Russian olives by the slough. I climb up the hill, Lucy still with me, until I get to the rock. Lida comes up behind me.

We don't say anything for a minute. Then Lida looks down at me.

"You're going to do it, aren't you?" she says.

I nod.

"It will keep him happy. It'll make him well again," I say.

Lida sighs.

"I don't know if it works that way, Jake."

We turn to watch a car drive up the long dirt road to the house. Dr. Miller's car.

Lida leans over to pat Lucy. Lucy turns and begins to walk back down the hill to the house.

"I just don't know," says Lida behind me.

Dr. Miller's red car is small and dusty from driving on dirt roads.

"Hello, Lucy," she says, bending down to stroke Lucy.

"How's he doing?"

"He's not acting like Billy," I say.

Dr. Miller nods.

"He's sick. We'll see if he calls me Chickie," she says.

Together we walk up the porch stairs and into the house. I open the kitchen door for Dr. Miller, and she pats me on the head when she goes by, a soft pat that makes me feel better for some reason.

"Mama's in Billy's room," I say.

Lucy and Dr. Miller disappear down the hallway.

Lida gets two glasses of water and ice from the refrigerator. She hands me a glass.

We sit at the kitchen table. It is quiet until Mama comes into the kitchen with Dr. Miller. Dr. Miller goes to the phone and dials. Mama looks pale, almost as pale as Billy looks.

"Billy will be better off in the hospital. We can keep an eye on him night and day," says Dr. Miller.

And then Papa and Jesse are there, too.

Papa puts his arms around Mama.

"He'll be close by, Charlotte," he says. "We can visit him every day."

Dr. Miller hangs up the phone.

"The ambulance is on its way," she says.

"What about Lucy?" I ask suddenly.

Dr. Miller looks at me.

"There are rules, Jake," she says softly.

"Rules?" I say loudly. "Those are *your* rules."

"Stop, Jake," says Papa.

"What about *Billy*'s rules?" I say.

I know I will begin to cry, the second time in two days. Mama is already crying.

"Billy has a rule about Lucy," I say. "They have to be together. Lucy came to Billy! That's Billy's rule."

Dr. Miller stares at me. She reaches over and takes my hand, and we hear the ambulance coming up the dirt road.

"That's Billy's rule," I say again very softly before Dr. Miller puts her arms around me.

9

The Pact

Lucy stands next to Billy's bed and stares at the stretcher, something new in Billy's bedroom. Mama keeps her hand on Lucy's head.

"Hello, Mae. Hi, Robbie," Mama says to the EMTs.

"Hi, Lottie. How are you feeling, Billy?" Mae stops when she sees Lucy.

"Is she friendly?"

Billy nods.

"She is just protecting me," he whispers.

Mae smiles.

"Well, tell her we are protecting you, too, Billy," she says.

Billy beckons to me, and I come into the room.

Mae and Robbie shift Billy from his bed to the stretcher. Billy pulls me closer.

"You take care of Lucy," he whispers. "You sleep in my bed and she'll be all right. Not happy, but all right."

"Your bed?"

I don't want to sleep in Billy's bed. That's

Billy's bed, not mine. Billy should be there. Not me.

"Promise me, Jake?"

Billy looks at me sternly.

"I promise," I say.

Billy pats my hand.

They take Billy through the kitchen, where Lida, Jesse, and Papa are standing.

"We'll come see you," says Papa.

"Bring decent food," says Billy, trying to be funny.

"Not a bad idea," says Dr. Miller, smiling, opening the door for Robbie and Mae.

We all walk out onto the porch as they open the doors to the ambulance and put Billy in.

"I'll call you later," says Dr. Miller, getting into her car. "You can visit starting at seven."

The ambulance goes off. We stand, still and quiet, and then suddenly Lucy leaps off the porch.

Jesse makes a grab for her collar, but she dodges him.

She is off down the road, following the dust of the ambulance.

"Lucy!" calls Mama.

Lucy doesn't stop or look around, but the ambulance stops.

"Go get her, Jake," says Papa. "Take a rope from inside the barn."

I run off to the barn and then down the road.

Robbie stands by the ambulance, waiting.

"That happens a lot," he says. "That dog loves Billy. She'll try to get away again."

"Come on, girl," I say, realizing that I sound like Billy. I tie the rope to Lucy's collar.

The ambulance goes off. Lucy pulls, trying to run off again, but I hold her. I turn around and pull her. She's strong, and she keeps looking back to the ambulance going off. But after a while she turns and follows me. Then she walks next to me all the way home, unhappily, her tail down.

Papa is back in the fields with Jesse. I walk up the stairs to the porch and into the kitchen. Only Lida is there.

I can hear Mama down the hall, rustling around in Billy's room.

I take the rope off Lucy and hang it on a hook. Lida puts her arms around Lucy and pets her.

"Jake?" Lida says, tears at the edges of her eyes.

"What? And don't cry."

Lida lifts her shoulders and wipes her eyes with the back of her hand.

"I have a sod cutter," she says very softly.

Lida and I sit on Billy's bed. Lucy stretches out, her head on Billy's pillow. The bedroom door is closed.

There's a soft knock and Jesse comes in.

"If I open the door, Lucy goes to the kitchen and wants out," I tell him.

"She'd go to the hospital," says Jesse.

Jesse sits on the bed, too.

"All right," says Jesse.

"All right what?" asks Lida.

"All right I'll help," says Jesse. "You can't do it by yourselves."

No one says anything. Then Jesse adds, "Plus, I want to do it."

"A pact," says Lida.

"A pact," says Jesse. "It won't be easy."

"Billy says doing anything worth doing is never easy," I say.

"Yeah," says Jesse with a smile. "Billy would say that."

He holds up his hand. Lida puts her hand next to it. I put my hand up, too.

Lucy gets up and looks at us with wide eyes.

"No," says Jesse to Lucy. "It's just us here. Billy's at the hospital."

He says it as if Lucy will understand.

Lucy stares at Jesse.

"Give me five, Lucy," says Jesse.

He holds up his hand, and Lucy puts up her paw, too.

"I taught her that," says Jesse.

"*I* taught her that!" I say.

"Wait," says Lida. "I taught her that!"

We laugh.

Lucy sits down again, rolls over.

She yawns her whiny dog yawn.

It's quiet again.

10

Angel Dog

Mama brushes her hair. Papa stands by the door, waiting. Lida and Jesse are doing their chores and Papa's, too. I am going to the hospital to see Billy.

The phone rings. I'm closest to the phone, and Mama nods at me.

"Hello."

"Jake?"

It's Dr. Miller.

"Bring Lucy."

She hangs up.

I stare at the phone for a minute, then I smile.

"What?" says Mama.

"Dr. Miller says bring Lucy."

"That Billy," she says.

"Want to go for a ride, Lucy?" she asks.

Lucy's ears prick up. She runs to the door.

"Take the rope, Jake. I don't trust Lucy," says Papa.

Lucy gives Papa a look as if she says, *Who, me? Not trustworthy? I'm your best friend.*

It's dusk when we ride to the hospital. I

sit in the back with Lucy. She looks out the window eagerly—looking for a man with a bush of white hair, looking for Billy.

When we get to the hospital, Lucy stands up in the backseat and wags her tail. *She knows.*

I've said it out loud because Mama nods.

"She does."

We get out with Lucy and walk through the front door. It's a low hospital, only one floor. The hall lights are on.

"Wait!" says the woman at the desk. "That's a dog. You can't bring her . . ."

Lucy pulls loose and runs down the hall— past doctors and nurses and visitors, past a steel cart with medicines—the rope trailing behind her.

"Lucy!" I call, chasing after her.

She turns into a room and we follow.

Billy's room.

When we get there, Lucy is up on the bed with Billy.

"Well, you found the room without any trouble," says Dr. Miller, standing next to the bed.

"Lucy did," says Mama.

Billy smiles. He has oxygen tubes in his nose, and his arm is hooked up to a machine.

He looks tired, but his face isn't so pale.

Lucy looks up at Dr. Miller.

"No, you can't stay here tonight," she says. "Rules," she adds, and looks at me. "But you can visit tomorrow again. *My* rules."

I smile at Dr. Miller.

Before we leave, Lucy visits other rooms— other sick people smiling at her, stroking her head.

"I should hire Lucy," says Dr. Miller.

"She's an angel dog," says Billy. "And don't you forget that."

"I'm thinking you're right," says Dr. Miller. "I like Angel Dog. She should visit every day."

"And she will do that, Chickie," says Billy.

Dr. Miller looks at me.

"He's better, don't you think?"

I nod. Billy has called her Chickie.

We watch Billy eat Mama's chicken soup.

We watch Billy take his medicine.

There's only one thing left.

It's night when we drive home again, but the moon is full, lighting our way home. Papa has even forgotten to put on the car's headlights. Lucy sleeps with her head on my lap, somehow comforted to have seen Billy for a short visit.

When we drive up the dirt road to our house, I see our small tractor in the side field by the slough, its headlights on.

"What's that?" asks Mama. "*Who's* that?"

Papa shakes his head.

"Looks like Lida."

I smile. I know it's Lida.

When Papa stops the car, I take Lucy on her rope and run up the hill, past the slough, past the granary.

I stop when I get to the field. Lucy sits.

Lida is cutting sod.

11

Poetry

I sleep with Lucy in Billy's bed because I promised. She sleeps next to me, sometimes lifting her head to peer at me as if to say *You're not the one I love. You're all right. But not the one I love.* Sometimes she moves on the bed so she can look out the window into the dark. *What does she see there?*

I wonder if she dreams.

I have many dreams.

My dreams are about Billy.

Lida and Jesse and I cut sod every day, shaping the bricks so they are all the same. We cut until we have hundreds. We move them to a wagon, and Lida pulls the wagon with the tractor to where the Russian olive bushes are.

"Why here?" asks Jesse.

I've cut away some of the Russian olive bushes. I point to where Billy's old sod house is. I don't need to say anything. Jesse knows.

"Billy's house," says Jesse.

I nod.

"I'm going to use that corner for the new house," I say.

Jesse smiles.

"Billy will like that. It's poetic."

"Poetic?"

"Old house, new house," says Jesse. "Poetry."

I don't know about that. But Jesse knows. He reads roomfuls of books.

"Poetry?" I ask him.

Jesse nods.

"Poetry," he says.

And we begin to build, the three of us. There's still water in the slough. Jesse hauls up water so we can make good mud to put between the sod bricks. Mama and Papa come up to watch, bringing Lucy on her rope leash.

"I can help," says Papa.

And we let him.

Mama sits on the rock, Lucy next to her, watching.

Jesse, who has read all about sod houses, teaches us to make the walls thick. He teaches us how to pile the bricks in double rows to strengthen the walls. He measures the house print that we have staked out.

"You'll have room for a bed, a chair, and a stove. Do we have a stove? And two windows."

"I have some old barn windows," says

Papa, piling up sod bricks and putting mud in between the bricks. "We can buy a stove for Billy."

"How long will it take to build the house?" asks Mama.

It's now four feet tall. We've left a door opening so Billy can look out over the slough.

"I don't know," I say.

"How long will Billy be in the hospital?" Jesse asks.

"Can we surprise him when he gets out?" asks Lida.

Mama shrugs.

"Dr. Miller thinks three, maybe four

more days," she says.

"Then that's how long it will take," says Jesse.

I look at Jesse.

"Poetry," I say.

"Yep," says Jesse. "Get to work."

12

The Secret

Every night I sleep with Lucy. And I come to understand something. Lucy likes me. She knows I like her. But she knows that I don't need her. Billy needs her. So she waits every day for us to take her in the car to visit Billy.

In the morning she patiently watches the

hummingbirds at the feeders. She patiently waits as we feed her breakfast and we eat our food.

At the hospital the rules have changed. Lucy is allowed in the front door and down the hallway to Billy's room. The woman at the front desk waves her hand and lets us by with Lucy, though I don't think she likes it much.

"Angel Dog," says Billy when Lucy comes into the room and jumps up on his bed.

Lucy rubs her head against Billy.

"She's rubbing her scent on me," he says. "I belong to her."

Billy looks better every day.

"What is going on at home?" he asks.

We make up things about home. And none of us—Jesse or Lida or Mama or I—tell him that we're building him a sod house.

"I'll be home in two days," says Billy. "Right, Chickie?" he asks Dr. Miller.

She laughs.

"We'll see. I want your breathing to be better. We'll see."

Dr. Miller knows about our sod house.

"I have to get home. We have a sod house to build," says Billy.

"What do you mean 'we'?" asks Dr. Miller. "You can't build anything for a while."

"Well, *they* will," says Billy, waving his

hand at us. "Right?"

Billy peers at us and we are silent.

"Lida, how's the sod-cutting research going?"

"Fine," says Lida. "I need a little more time. Rubin is going to lend me his cutter."

Lida's lie makes her blush, but Billy doesn't see it. Rubin's sod cutter has worked very well. The house walls are straight and very thick and over our head. The roof will come next.

"That's great, Lida," says Billy. "Get ready; I'll be home soon."

"Oh, we'll be ready," says Jesse, his face as peaceful and innocent as I've ever seen.

"We'll certainly be ready."

Billy takes my hand.

"The hummingbirds still there?"

"Yes. I clean out their feeders every other day, like you showed me. Lucy watches."

"Of course she does," says Billy, leaning back on his pillows. "Summer's nearly over. In the fall they'll go."

I don't know why, but I feel goose bumps up my arms.

"They come back, though," I say quickly.

"They do. Where's your papa?" asks Billy.

"Chores," says Jesse.

Papa is home building the wooden frame for the roof of the sod house.

Billy looks at Lucy.

"Chores? What do *you* know?" he asks. "You know a secret, Lucy? Tell me."

Lucy looks at me, then at Jesse and Lida. She *does* know our secret. I stare at Billy, trying to see if he's kidding or not.

"Chicken soup?" asks Mama.

"You bet," says Billy.

"You bet," says Dr. Miller.

The secret is forgotten.

13

A Good Sign

Two days before Billy's supposed to come home from the hospital we finish the roof rafters. Jesse and Lida climb down their ladders. There is a sudden quiet; even the wind is quiet as we look at the house. No rustling in the Russian olives.

Lucy watches, sitting quietly by the front door of the sod house. She doesn't need a leash anymore. Mama thinks it is because she goes to visit Billy every day. I think it is because she knows Billy will be in this house soon.

Mama pours lemonade for us all.

"Almost done," says Papa in a soft voice.

Jesse wipes his face with the back of his hand.

"The roof next," he says.

"Leave one piece," says Mama quietly.

We all look at her.

"For Billy."

Lida nods.

"I hope," she says, imitating Billy's voice, "the roof sod grass is pointing to the sky!"

She sounds so much like Billy that Lucy

looks up at her, tilting her head.

Later that morning we nearly finish the roof. I've stripped the leaves off the Russian olives I cleared so that I can climb up to put a layer of branches over the sod. Now Mama can whitewash the walls we've made smooth inside.

We all go inside and stand in the sod house. It is empty except for us and the little yellow woodstove Papa has bought.

"You visit Billy without me today," Mama says. "Lida and I have finishing work to do."

"Finishing? What do you mean?" I say.

"You'll see," says Mama. "Shoo, shoo." She waves us off.

This makes Lucy bark, and we laugh.

"Laugher in this house," says Mama, smiling. "That's a good sign."

We laugh more. A good sign.

At the hospital Billy is feisty. At least that's what Dr. Miller says.

Billy is sitting on the side of the bed, his legs dangling, petting Lucy.

"Bring that man some clothes tomorrow and take him away," Dr. Miller says.

"You love me, Chickie," says Billy. "You know that."

"I do," says Dr. Miller, "along with my husband, my two children, my dog, and my goat, Rosemary."

"You never told me you have a goat!" says Billy, making us all laugh.

Billy walks down the hospital hallway in his bathrobe with Lucy and his cane, looking into rooms, waving at people.

"I'm leaving tomorrow," he says. "You'll miss me."

"Did you finish the house?" whispers Dr. Miller.

"Yes," I whisper. "We left the last piece of sod off the roof. For Billy."

Dr. Miller smiles.

"Good thought," she says. "I'll come out tomorrow afternoon to check on him."

"And to see the sod house," I say.

"Of course to see the sod house!" she repeats.

When we get home, Lucy jumps out of the car and runs up the hill to the sod house as if she knows something. And she does.

The sod house door is open, and when we step inside, we see that the walls are smooth and white. Mama and Lida have hung two pictures: an old one of the farm when Billy owned it, and one of the slough. There is a bed with a yellow quilt, a small table with an oil lamp on it, and a vase of flowers picked from Mama's garden. The rocking chair Billy's mama brought all the way from Europe sits near the door so Billy can sit in it and look at his slough. On the floor is Mama's favorite red Oriental rug with green trees and golden deer on it.

The sod house is beautiful.

Lucy lies down on the rug as if she's home. And she is.

14

Rusty Cage

The day.

Somehow Lucy knows. She wakes with the hummingbirds, scratches at the bedroom door; and when I let her out, she runs to the car. She sits in the sunlight, looking at me.

"Breakfast first," I call to her.

Slowly, Lucy comes back into the house

and waits by her breakfast dish.

Mama is surprised to see me in the kitchen.

"I'll bet Lucy woke you," she says.

"Good bet."

I pour cereal into my bowl.

Mama spoons food into Lucy's dish and sits down at the table.

"You did it, Jake," she says.

"We all did it," I say.

"But you made it happen," Mama says.

"We're kindred souls," I say, shrugging my shoulders.

Mama smiles. "You are."

Lucy gets up and sits next to Mama. Mama pets her.

I eat my cereal.

The phone rings.

Mama answers.

"Hello?"

Mama laughs.

"Okay."

She hangs up.

"Billy says, don't forget his shoes."

The phone rings again.

Mama raises her eyebrows at me and answers again.

"Hello?"

She grins at Lucy.

"Of course."

She hangs up.

"Don't forget Lucy," we say together, laughing.

At the hospital Billy dresses faster than I've ever seen. He slicks down his white hair so that even Lucy stares at him.

"Yes," I tell Lucy. "It's really Billy."

"Where's everyone?" asks Billy.

"They're at home, working," I say.

"Working at what?" asks Billy with a sly smile.

Mama and I don't say anything.

"Working at what?" Billy repeats.

"All right," I say. "I confess. We have staked out the sod house."

Billy slaps his knee.

"I knew it! Let's go. Have to get home and build it. Lottie, if you just get one of those old lawn chairs out, I can sit there and tell them how to do it."

Mama smiles.

"I can do that, Billy," she says.

Dr. Miller pokes her head in the doorway.

"Go home, Billy," she says. "I'll be out to see you this afternoon."

"Bye, Chickie," says Billy.

And we're off, Billy waving good-bye to the woman at the front desk, who is glad to be rid of him and Lucy. Billy sits in the backseat with Lucy, both of them looking out the windows.

"Turn on the radio, Jake," says Billy. "We need some music."

And we ride all the way home to the music of Johnny Cash singing:

"... *gonna break my rusty cage and run* ..."

Billy smiles.

"I like that song," he says.

We turn down the long dirt road past our meadows, past the cows and Billy the calf, past the horses. We come into the yard, and Billy opens the back door before we've stopped.

"Let's go," he says.

But Lucy jumps out ahead of Billy and

starts up the hill to the slough. She turns and waits for him.

Mama takes his arm and together they follow Lucy.

"Jake, you coming?" says Billy, making me smile.

"I'm coming, Billy."

And then Billy stops.

The house stands with the sun on it, outlining every brick. Jesse is up on the ladder, finishing laying the branches. The Russian olive bushes that I've left sit at the corner where Billy's first sod house was. But, of course, Billy doesn't know that yet.

Billy's mouth opens and closes. He looks

sideways at Mama. Then they walk closer. Billy's old lawn chair sits on the small flat rise where the house is built. Jesse turns, and Lida and Papa come around the house. Billy sits in the chair.

"That roof sod goes with the grass part facing the sky, you know!" he says, making us all laugh. "And"— he points to the corner of the sod house—"that's my old house, isn't it? *Isn't it?*"

That is when the tears come down Billy's face.

15

Old Home, New Home

We have never seen Billy cry in our whole lives, Jesse and Lida and I. But Mama and Papa don't seem upset. Mama smiles actually.

"We left the last piece of roof sod for you, Billy," Papa says.

Billy looks at the ladder.

"You do it, Jake," he says softly.

"Me?"

"You."

I take the piece of sod and climb up the ladder.

"Grass to the sky," says Billy.

I smile and put the last sod piece in place. I feel a little shiver when I do it. Like it is something important and final.

"Why don't you go inside the house, Billy?" says Mama.

She opens the door and hands Billy his cane.

"Go inside."

Billy is very quiet when he walks into the sod house. He looks at the pictures on the wall, the bed with the quilt, and his mama's rocking chair. Lucy jumps up on the bed, turns around once, and lies down. Billy looks at us outside the house.

"Thank you all," he says.

Then he reaches out and shuts the door of the sod house, leaving the rest of us outside.

I look at Mama.

"He has to rest," she says. "And he has to think about all of this. Alone."

Billy has never closed the door on me before. Jesse touches my shoulder.

"Let's go eat pie," he says.

Jesse and I walk down the hill. He reaches out to tag me suddenly and then ducks out of the way when I try to tag him back. We laugh all the way down the hill, trying to tag each other. Lida catches up, and at the bottom of the hill we turn around and look up at the house, so peaceful in the afternoon light.

"He loves it," says Lida.

"He loves it," says Jesse.

Jesse puts his arm across my shoulders.

"Yes," I say.

Billy stays inside the sod house all afternoon. Papa goes out to the fields, and Mama cooks soup on the stove.

Dr. Miller's car comes down the dirt road, sending dust up behind it. She stops out front, lifts her black doctor's bag from the front seat, and comes into the kitchen.

"Billy?" she asks.

"Up in the sod house. With Lucy," says Mama.

Dr. Miller nods.

"Of course," she says. "I'll just take a walk up there."

"He cried," I tell her as she opens the door.

She stops.

"Of course," she repeats.

"I'll walk you up," says Lida.

And then they're gone.

I frown at Mama and Jesse.

"I don't understand anything," I say. "I

don't understand why Billy cried. I don't understand why he's in that sod house all by himself. With that dog," I add.

"Yes, you do," says Jesse, "even though you're just a kid. He cried because it was a gift. You were the one who gave Billy this gift. I'd never have done it on my own."

I stare at Jesse. I'm not sure he's ever said this many words to me before in his life. Then he says one more thing.

"And 'that dog' is his angel."

Mama turns from stirring the soup on the stove and smiles at Jesse.

"Once you thought that was crazy!" I say.

"I did," says Jesse. "But I don't think it's

crazy anymore. Not anymore," he repeats softly.

And then, before I can answer, the door swings open and Billy and Dr. Miller come in with Lucy.

"Now for the next thing, Jake," says Billy happily. "All I need is an outhouse!"

16

The Gift

The days go by. The nights are cooler. Soon it will be fall. And school.

I don't want the summer to end.

Billy spends days with Lucy in his sod house. Sometimes he invites me in, too. But it is Billy's house. As Jesse tells me, "You built it, but it is Billy's house. That's what a gift is."

In a way I have made something happen

that separates us. Billy and Lucy have their own space now. I didn't mean for that to happen.

"You built that sod house for Billy so he'd get well," Lida reminds me.

"And he did," I say.

Most nights Billy comes back to the farmhouse to eat dinner and sleep in his own bed.

"I think we should build another room or two," he says to me one night, "so you can have a room there, too."

I feel tears and can't speak.

Billy pats my head, one of his small taps that means "I love you."

Some days when it is cool outside, Billy builds a fire in his yellow stove. We have hot chocolate, all of us gathered around. There is, in the sod house, a smell of prairie and wildflowers and good earth.

"There is nothing like this in the whole wide world," says Billy. Then he looks over at us. "Heaven maybe," he says.

The hummingbirds still come to Billy's window feeders. Their young come, too, squeaking and swooping.

"They're filling up before they go south," says Billy. "I'll miss them when they're gone."

"You used to say that about your old sod house," I say to him. "That you missed it."

"I did, didn't I?" says Billy. "I have nothing much to miss anymore."

There is something sad about Billy that I don't understand.

"You're supposed to be happier," I say. "That's why we built your sod house."

Billy looks at me for a long time.

"I am happy," he says.

The day is warm for mid-September, though geese are flying high above. Fall is coming.

Billy has taken his cane and invited me for a walk around the slough with Lucy.

"This will fill up with water," he says. "The ducks will come."

I smile. Billy is telling me things I know because I live here.

Some of the bushes by the slough have changed to yellow. Some of the fields are yellow, too. We walk down the hill, where Billy speaks to the calf Billy, who is very peppy today.

"Hello, kiddo. Hello, girls."

The horses run along the fence with us, hoping Billy has carrots. Which he does.

"I'm tired," says Billy. "Tell your mama I'll be there for dinner after my nap."

"I will."

I watch him go up the hill with Lucy. Lucy walks ahead, then stops and waits for Billy.

I walk back toward the house.

"Hey?"

Billy calls to me.

He looks down at me. Lucy looks, too.

"I'm happy," he calls. "I'm happy, Jake."

I wave. He waves back, smiling.

He doesn't close the door of the sod house.

Lida is setting the table for dinner. Jesse is sampling something out of a pot on the stove. Papa washes up.

"Billy will be here," I say. "In a while."

Mama nods.

"We'll go ahead without him. He'll be along."

After a while we sit down for dinner, six places at the table. Five of us there.

And then there is a scratch at the door.

I get up and open it.

Lucy stands there looking at me. She has never scratched at the door before. Ever.

"Lucy?"

I turn and see Mama getting up, almost in slow motion. Papa moves to the door.

"Lucy?" he repeats.

And I'll never forget the sound of his voice. It is almost a cry.

I know right away. I know.

Papa runs up the hill to the sod house, Mama behind him.

Jesse and Lida and I sit at the table.

We know.

Lucy doesn't follow Mama and Papa. She stands, looking at us, her eyes steady and large.

Billy dies in his mama's rocking chair, leaning back as if he were napping. The door is open to the slough. The quilt on the bed is mussed, as if a dog has been lying there.

The sun goes down.

17

Leaving

We never see Lucy again. But a few days later Jesse brings me a newspaper story of a dog who has visited a woman's sick mother in the next town, making her life much better. There is no picture of the dog.

"This dog is a jewel," the woman says. "She makes my mother's last days happy."

"Angel Dog," says Jesse.

Sometimes I think Lucy comes back to the sod house. Sometimes I think there is a shadow there, the door left ajar, a small dent in the quilt.

But I never see her.

Jesse and Lida and I sit in the sod house.

"I built the sod house so Billy would get well and stay," I say to Lida. "Remember?"

Lida nods.

"But what you really did was give him the place he wanted so he could leave," Jesse says.

Geese honk high in the sky outside.

And the morning after we bury Billy, the hummingbirds are gone, too.